# WAKE UP, CITY!

*For Dorothy Briley—with many thanks!*

First Edition   1  2  3  4  5  6  7  8  9  10

Library of Congress Cataloging in Publication Data
Tresselt, Alvin R. Wake up, city!/by Alvin Tresselt; illustrated by Carolyn Ewing.     p.
cm. Summary: Describes all the many things that begin to happen as morning comes to the
city. ISBN 0-688-08652-7.—ISBN 0-688-08653-5 (lib. bdg.) [1. Day—Fiction.
2.  City and town life—Fiction.]   I. Ewing, C. S. ill.    II. Title. PZ7.T732Wak
1990     [E]—dc20
89-45901 CIP AC

# ALVIN TRESSELT

# WAKE UP, CITY!

## PICTURES BY CAROLYN EWING

LOTHROP, LEE & SHEPARD BOOKS   NEW YORK

Under the stars the city sleeps.
Only the police officers are about, walking their beat.
Only an alley cat, prowling a backyard fence.
Only a mother, rocking her baby back to sleep.

Then slowly the eastern sky begins to brighten.
Here a light goes on...there a light goes on,
as people stir and waken.

The city sparrows begin to cheep.
And the ducks on the pond in the park
call to one another across the black water.

The city is waking in the dim dawn light,
and the tops of tall buildings glow
in the first rays of the rising sun.
The police officers sniff the fresh morning air.
"It looks like another great day!" they say to each other.

In the garages buses are ready for the day's work.
The gas tanks are full and the windshields are clean.
The bus drivers straighten their caps and hop aboard,
and off go the big buses, rolling down the street.

In the harbor a great freighter from across the world
comes in on the morning tide.
Tugboats and harbor patrols
are all ready for a busy day.

# CHAPTER ONE

# WHAT IS GEOTHERMAL ENERGY?

The drill operators watch their equipment. Their rig has been running for 40 days. Its drill bit is almost 2 miles (3.2 km) below Earth's surface. It spins and churns, cutting through rock. Its target is an underground steam field.

There are sensors on the end of the drill. They detect heat. Suddenly the temperature spikes. The drill operators get ready. Deep underground, the drill

Drilling for geothermal exploration requires heavy equipment and several workers.

The Calistoga plant in the Geysers is one of the largest US geothermal power plants.

breaks through to a pocket of superheated steam. A thick white blast of steam shoots into the air. It roars like a jet engine. The drillers rush over to seal the wellhead.

The superheated steam from this well is 575 degrees Fahrenheit (300°C). It will be sent through a turbine. As the turbine spins, it generates electricity. The well is in California in an area called the Geysers. Heat is stored below the ground in this region. The heat from the Geysers supplies enough energy to run more than 20 power plants.

## Earth's Hot Core

Heat stored underground is called geothermal energy. *Geo* and *therme* are the Greek words for "Earth" and "heat." Earth's core can reach 10,800 degrees Fahrenheit (6,000°C). This is about the same temperature as the surface of the sun.

Some of the Earth's inner heat is left over from when the planet formed. This happened more than 4.5 billion years ago. Some of it comes from radioactive elements naturally found in rock. The elements release heat as they decay.

Heat from Earth's core flows out toward the surface. Some becomes trapped in cracks and pores filled with water. The water warms up. It becomes a reservoir of geothermal energy. Some geothermal reservoirs are close to the surface. People can drill into them and use the heat.

### Geothermal Reservoirs

Some heat from the Earth's core is transferred to underground water. Water falls as rain. It seeps underground. The water is held in cracks and pores of rock. When the water is trapped under a layer of solid rock, it forms a geothermal reservoir. What are some ways this energy source can be put to use?

The rate at which temperatures increase deeper in the Earth is known as the geothermal gradient. The average geothermal gradient in most places is approximately 45 degrees Fahrenheit (25°C) for every 0.62 miles (1 km) of depth. In places with geothermal reservoirs, it is much higher. It may be more than 180 degrees Fahrenheit (100°C) per 0.62 miles (1 km).

## Renewable and Nonrenewable

Energy is a property of an object that can be stored or used to carry out work. Energy heats and cools buildings. It powers electronics and cars. It can come from renewable or nonrenewable sources. Wind, solar, and geothermal energy are examples of renewable energy. They will not run out. Fossil fuels such as coal, oil, and natural gas are nonrenewable. These fuels are burned for energy. They cannot be easily replaced. There is another downside to these fuels. They create dangerous pollution. However, they are easy to access and contain large amounts of energy. They are currently the world's main source of energy.

Fossil fuel power plants release gases that harm the environment.

# Clean Geothermal Energy

Geothermal energy has many upsides. It is a natural and renewable source of energy. It is also plentiful, reliable, and clean. Geothermal energy can reduce our dependence on fossil fuels. But unlike solar or wind power, it is available any time. It can be used day or night, no matter the weather.

Geothermal energy has many uses. It can heat or cool buildings. It can also be used to generate electricity. Hundreds of geothermal plants around the world are in use. They power approximately 11 million homes.

## Finding Geothermal Energy

Geothermal activity can sometimes be easy to see. It can reach Earth's surface in the form of volcanoes, geysers, and hot springs. But most geothermal energy is deep underground. Geologists use many methods to find hidden reservoirs. They study maps and pictures. They test the chemistry of soil and water. They take many measurements. Then they drill small, deep exploration wells. They use these wells to collect rock samples and check temperatures. If the results are good, they drill larger production wells.

Still, that amounts to less than 1 percent of the world's electricity. Approximately 66 percent of the world's electricity is made by burning fossil fuels.

Geothermal is sometimes overshadowed by other energy alternatives. These include solar, wind, and hydropower. The problem is geology. To use geothermal energy, a place needs hot rock close to the surface. This is rare. Such areas exist on only 10 percent of the planet. In most places, these resources are miles below the surface.

Scientists are working on new ways to harvest geothermal energy. They want to make it easy to tap into this energy source. New research may help geothermal energy become a key part of our energy future.

Dr. Euan Mearns is a geologist and Honorary Research Fellow at the University of Aberdeen, Scotland. He wrote about why geothermal energy has been less popular than other sources:

> *Installing solar panels or onshore wind turbines is a comparatively simple and predictable undertaking, but like oil and gas, geothermal requires exploratory drilling and testing to confirm the presence of a resource, more drilling and testing to determine size and productivity and ultimately to a wellfield and power plant that's specifically tailored to the resource (there is no one-size-fits-all design). All this takes time and money and involves risk, and as a rule investors will shy away from risk if they can avoid it.*

> Source: Euan Mearns. "Why Geothermal Energy Will Remain a Small Player." Oilprice.com. Oilprice.com, July 1, 2015. Web. Accessed June 30, 2016.

## Changing Minds

Imagine you are a geothermal energy developer. Write a short essay trying to convince investors that the risks of developing geothermal energy are worth it. Make sure you explain your opinion. Include facts and details that support your reasons.

# CHAPTER TWO

# GEOTHERMAL, PAST AND PRESENT

**G**eothermal energy exists in many different forms. It may be stored underground in water or rocks. It may come to the surface as steam, hot water, or lava. Each form differs in temperature, depth, and how it can be used. Over time, three ways to use geothermal energy have developed. They are direct use, geothermal heat pumps, and as an energy source to make electricity.

Geothermal energy can be seen in hot springs and geysers.

# Direct Use of Geothermal Energy

When geothermal heat is used straight from the ground, it is called direct use. For centuries, people have been using hot springs and pools for bathing, cooking, and heating.

Thousands of years ago, Native Americans bathed in geothermal springs. These waters often had religious meaning. They were believed to have healing powers. There is evidence that the ancient Chinese and Romans also used geothermal hot spots. So did people in Iceland, Japan, and Turkey.

People later discovered they could use geothermal energy to heat buildings. In the 1890s, the residents of Boise, Idaho, started to heat their homes with water from geothermal wells. A few decades later, Icelanders set up large-scale systems to heat many buildings.

Today, people continue to put geothermal energy to direct use. It is a source of household hot water. It heats greenhouses and fish farms. It is used to dry

Animals and people alike make use of the geothermal heat from hot springs.

lumber and process fruits and vegetables. It is also piped under roads to melt snow and ice. In Iceland, Japan, and other countries, hot springs are popular tourist destinations.

## Geothermal Heat Pumps

Geothermal hot water or steam is often unavailable. However, the ground still stores some geothermal energy. Just a few feet below the surface, the temperature is stable. It stays at around 50 degrees Fahrenheit (10°C) no matter what season it is.

In the 1940s, researcher Carl Nielsen developed a way to use the ground's temperature to heat or cool a home or building. His system is called a geothermal heat pump. It brings heat into the building in the winter. It carries heat away in the summer. Geothermal heat pumps have become the second most common way to use geothermal resources. The first is generating electricity.

## How Geothermal Heat Pumps Work

Geothermal heat pumps heat or cool buildings. A closed loop of pipe is filled with water or another fluid. Most of the loop is buried in the ground. The rest goes into a house or building. As fluid circulates through the system, it transfers heat from the ground to an indoor heat pump. The heat is then sent throughout the building. In the summer, the same system can move heat from the building into the ground. This has a cooling effect. Geothermal heat pump systems are very energy efficient. They can be installed almost anywhere in the world.

Steam rises from the ground in vents in Larderello, Italy.

## Making Electricity

In the early 1900s, people began using geothermal energy as a source for making electricity. This usually requires temperatures that are higher than those involved in direct use.

The first geothermal electricity was generated in Larderello, Italy. This area has rare conditions. Large amounts of hot steam billow out of the ground. Starting in 1904, the steam was used to power a generator. It made enough electricity to light up five light bulbs. This was the first time geothermal energy was used to make electricity. A power plant was built. In 1913 the power plant started to serve customers. Today, power plants in Larderello make 1.6 percent of Italy's electricity.

Other geothermal power plants followed. In 1958 a small plant was built in Wairakei, New Zealand. Within the next few years, projects were started in Pathe, Mexico, and in northern California at the Geysers.

Today, 24 countries have geothermal power

## The Ring of Fire

Earth's outer layer is called the crust. It is made up of pieces called plates. The Pacific plate is the largest. It lies beneath the Pacific Ocean. Along its edge is a 25,000-mile (40,000-km) area called the Ring of Fire. This is where much of Earth's geothermal activity can be found. Volcanic eruptions and earthquakes are common. So are hot springs, bubbling mud, and geysers. Here, Earth's inner heat makes its way close to the surface. Many geothermal power plants are located along the Ring of Fire.

plants. They include the Philippines, Kenya, Japan, Iceland, Russia, and China. The United States leads the world in the amount of power generated. Every year, it generates 17 billion kilowatt-hours of geothermal electricity. Still, this makes up just 0.4 percent of US electricity.

## EXPLORE ONLINE

Chapter Two focuses on the history of geothermal energy around the world. The website below provides a timeline of geothermal energy use. How is the information from the website the same as the information in Chapter Two? What new information did you learn from the website?

## Geothermal Energy Timeline

mycorelibrary.com/geothermal-energy

# CHAPTER THREE

# HARVESTING GEOTHERMAL ENERGY

The most important way people use geothermal resources is to generate electricity. Geothermal power plants need steam or hot water to do this. To access these resources, workers drill wells. They can reach a mile (1.6 km) or more below Earth's surface. Steam or hot water is piped to the surface. Their heat is used as an energy source.

Geothermal power plants must be located near accessible geothermal resources, which are rare in most parts of the world.

## The Basics

All geothermal power plants have parts in common. The job of these parts is to turn one type of energy into another. Heat, or thermal energy, is used to drive a turbine. The turbine is connected to a generator. The generator converts the mechanical energy of motion into electricity.

Once steam passes through the turbine, it cools and turns back into water. The water may be used in the plant's cooling system. Or it may be pumped back into the geothermal source.

### Really Renewable?

Geothermal energy is a renewable resource. However, heat can be removed from the ground too quickly. The temperature of a geothermal reservoir can eventually cool down. Also, the water that carries the heat can be used up. The steam pressure at the dry steam plants in Larderello, Italy, has dropped by 25 percent since the 1950s. The pressure at the Geysers has also dropped. In many cases, water is injected back into the reservoir. This helps a cooling geothermal site last longer. However, this process can also cause small earthquakes.

Geothermal plants convert the spinning motion of
turbines into electricity.

Workers in a control room monitor a flash steam power plant.

There are three main types of geothermal power plants. They are dry steam, flash steam, and binary cycle plants. Each uses a different temperature range of steam or water.

## Dry Steam Plants

The first geothermal power plants in the world used natural steam. This is a high-temperature geothermal resource. Superheated dry steam is so hot it has no liquid water. It is the easiest form of geothermal energy to convert into electricity. But only a few locations have the right conditions for it.

In a dry steam plant, natural underground steam is piped out of a geothermal well to a power plant. The steam powers a turbine. This in turn is used to generate electricity.

## Case Study: Iceland

Iceland has a lot of geothermal energy below its surface. It has at least 25 active volcanoes. There are also many hot springs and geysers. Iceland has become a major user of geothermal energy. Almost all of the country's electricity, heat, and hot water come from geothermal resources. Systems of pipes carry hot water to homes. Pools, spas, city sidewalks, greenhouses, and fisheries are all heated with natural hot water. Iceland's capital, Reykjavik, has become one of the top clean energy cities in the world.

Italy's Valle Secolo geothermal power station is a dry steam plant.

Power plants in Larderello, Italy, and at the Geysers are dry steam plants. Other dry steam plants can be found in Japan and Indonesia.

## Flash Steam Plants

Flash steam power plants are more common than dry steam plants. Instead of pure steam, they use a mix of hot water and steam that is 320 degrees Fahrenheit (160°C) or higher. This makes them a moderate-temperature geothermal resource. High-pressure hot water is piped from geothermal wells into a flash steam power plant. When the water enters a low-pressure area, some of it turns into steam. This process is called flashing. The steam is then used to power a turbine and generate electricity.

Iceland has several flash steam geothermal power plants. They supply almost all of the country's electricity. The Philippines also uses flash steam power plants. The nation is second only to the United States in the amount of geothermal energy it produces. In all, almost two-thirds of geothermal power plants use a flash steam design.

## Binary Cycle Power Plants

Binary cycle plants use water that is 167 degrees Fahrenheit (75°C) or above. It is not hot enough to flash into steam. This makes it a low-temperature geothermal resource. The water is brought above

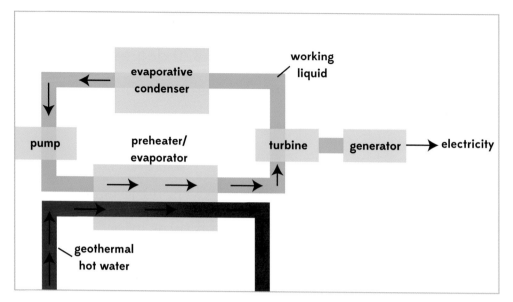

**Diagram of a Binary Cycle Geothermal Power Plant**
This diagram shows one method for converting geothermal energy to electric energy. What elements do you see that are common to all geothermal power plants? What parts are specific to a binary plant? When might a binary plant be the best approach?

ground in a pipe. It passes through a heat exchanger, where it heats another liquid in a separate pipe. The second liquid has a much lower boiling point than water. The heat turns this second liquid into a gas. This gas then drives a turbine and powers a generator to create electricity.

The gas cools and turns back into liquid. It can cycle around and be used over and over again.

The water in the pipe is recycled back to the ground. There it can be reheated and reused.

Binary cycle plants are not as efficient as the other two types of geothermal power plants. Still, many countries in the world have geothermal resources that will only work with this kind of plant. Some US plants use this system.

# CHAPTER FOUR

# WARMING UP THE FUTURE

There are huge amounts of thermal energy underground. But little can be used. Most of it is too deep or too spread out. To use geothermal activity for electricity production, three things are needed. They are hot rocks, cracks and pores, and water or steam. The rocks heat the water. Then the water moves through the cracks and pores.

The presence of high temperatures close to the surface is critical to most of today's geothermal technology.

It carries heat from deep hot zones to the surface. But many areas do not have all of these things.

In most parts of the world, there is hot rock several miles below the surface. But it is dry and can be difficult to reach. New techniques are being developed to access this heat and bring it to the surface. If these methods are successful, geothermal power plants could spread throughout the world. They could replace many fossil fuel plants.

## Enhanced Geothermal Systems

Scientists have been developing a system for geothermal sources that do not have enough

## Geothermal Pros and Cons

**Pros**

- It is available at all times.
- It is everywhere, if you drill deep enough.
- It is clean compared to fossil fuels.

**Cons**

- Geothermal systems can be very expensive.
- Drilling deep into heated rock is not easy.
- Reservoirs of geothermal energy can be depleted.

Geothermal research sites are investigating ways to improve geothermal energy equipment and processes.

cracks or water. It is called an enhanced geothermal system (EGS).

To develop an EGS, two wells are drilled into hot, dry rock. The wells are at least 300 feet (90 m) apart. They are up to 6 miles (10 km) deep. High-pressure cold water is injected into the first well. It makes

**35**

cracks in the rock. A network of cracks spreads between the two wells. Water is pumped down the first well. The hot rock heats it. Then the water is brought back up to the surface though the second well. It can now be used to generate electricity.

## Making Improvements

Drilling deep into hard rock can be extremely difficult. It is very time-consuming. It is tough to know what is going on so deep under the surface. And every well is different.

Drill bits wear out or break. Drilling can release explosive gas. It can also release other harmful substances. Drilling is also very expensive. It can cost as much as $20 million to drill a well. For an EGS project, drilling is often the largest cost.

Engineers and scientists are looking for ways to improve drilling. Many new ideas are being tested. One is known as an Earth Gun. It fires projectiles into the ground to make a well hole. The projectiles travel at up to 4,500 miles per hour (7,200 km/h)

Drill bits used to dig geothermal wells are extremely tough, but the harsh conditions underground can still wear them down.

and destroy everything in their path. This way of making wells could save time and money. However, it could potentially pose risks to the local geology and groundwater.

Another possible way to improve EGS is to replace the water with carbon dioxide. When carbon dioxide gas is placed under pressure, it turns to liquid. This liquid is better at carrying heat than water. The use of carbon dioxide can help produce electricity in more places at lower temperatures for less cost. It can save water resources. And unlike water, it will not dissolve harmful minerals.

## EGS and Earthquakes

EGS has some risks. Cracking rock and pumping water underground can cause earthquakes. In 2006 a geothermal project in Basel, Switzerland, caused an earthquake. The next year, more earthquakes occurred. A few were strong enough to damage buildings. In 2009 the project was brought to a stop.

The Soultz geothermal plant uses heat sources up to 3.1 miles (5 km) in depth.

## Testing in France

A full-scale EGS is operating in Soultz, France. Many countries are working together on the project. It began in 1986. In 2007 the first binary geothermal plant at Soultz was built. It can provide power to 1,500 homes.

Soultz is not the only project underway. Many countries, including Australia, Germany, Sweden, Japan, and the United States, are also working on EGS projects.

## Into the Future

World energy demands keep increasing. Fossil fuels such as coal, oil, and natural gas are used to produce most of the world's electricity. But at current rates, scientists estimate coal could run out in 200 years. Oil and natural gas may run out in just 60 years.

Renewable geothermal energy is a promising alternative. One study says there is enough geothermal energy to power the planet for thousands of years. If successful, EGS will be able to harvest geothermal energy in many new locations. Geothermal energy is likely to be an important part of the world's future energy supply.

Domenico Giardini is the director of the Swiss Seismological Service. He wrote about how using geothermal resources can increase the risk of earthquakes. He believes that openly discussing this issue will help support the future of geothermal as an energy source:

> It is now becoming clear to the public, local authorities, the geothermal industry and regulatory agencies that deep geothermal systems carry a small risk—as do most technologies in the energy sector. Dams can break, nuclear power plants may fail, carbon dioxide released from the oil and gas contributes to global warming, and EGS projects can create damage through induced earthquakes. The open question is whether or not society is able to find ways to balance and accept these risks. A well-informed discussion is needed to find out.

Source: Domenico Giardini. "Geothermal Quake Risks Must Be Faced." Nature. Nature, December 17, 2009. Web. Accessed July 1, 2016.

### Back It Up

The author of this passage is using evidence to support a point. Write a paragraph describing the point the author is making. Then write down two or three pieces of evidence the author uses to make the point.

- Geothermal energy is heat that comes from inside Earth. It is a natural and renewable source of energy.
- Using geothermal energy is much better for the environment than burning fossil fuels.
- People have been using geothermal energy for thousands of years and converting it to electrical energy for more than 100 years.
- In the United States, geothermal power plants can be found in California and other Western states.
- There are three main types of geothermal power plants. They are dry steam, flash steam, and binary cycle plants. Each uses water and steam in a different temperature range.
- Geothermal heat pumps use the constant temperatures found underground to heat and cool homes.
- With current technology, geothermal reservoirs are only easily accessible in a few regions around the planet.

- Reaching geothermal reservoirs underground can be expensive.
- Enhanced geothermal systems (EGS) are being developed. They turn underground areas with hot dry rock into usable sources of energy by introducing fluid and cracks.

## Another View

This book talks about geothermal energy and the ways it is used. Find another source on this topic. Write a short essay comparing and contrasting the new source's point of view with that of this book's author. What is the point of view of each author? How are they similar and why? How are they different and why?

## Take a Stand

Chapters One and Four outline some of the pros and cons of geothermal energy. Do you think the positives of developing geothermal energy as a power source outweigh the negatives? Or do you think efforts should be focused on other energy sources instead? Write an essay with at least three pieces of evidence to support your view. Be as specific as possible.

## Tell the Tale

Chapter Two discusses the hot springs of Iceland and Japan. Find another source with information about one of these springs. Write 200 words about a visit to the spring. Include the scientific details you have learned about geothermal springs from this book.

## Dig Deeper

After reading this book, what questions do you still have about geothermal energy? With an adult's help, find a few reliable sources that can help you answer your questions. Write a paragraph about what you learned.

# GLOSSARY

**crust**
Earth's outer layer

**drill bit**
a tool that attaches to the
end of a drill to break or
crush rock

**generator**
a machine that converts
mechanical energy into
electricity

**geologist**
a scientist who studies the
structure of Earth

**geyser**
a hot spring that shoots hot
water and steam into the air

**heat exchanger**
a device that transfers heat
from one fluid to another

**pores**
tiny holes that allow liquid or
gas to pass through

**reservoir**
an area where a supply of
water collects

**rig**
a structure that supports
equipment designed to drill
deep into the ground

**turbine**
an engine with rotor blades
that spin when water, steam,
wind, or gas passes across
them

**well**
a deep hole that has been
drilled into the ground

# LEARN MORE

## Books

Brennan, Linda Crotta. *Geothermal Power*. Ann Arbor, MI: Cherry Lake Publishing, 2013.

Mulder, Michelle. *Brilliant! Shining a Light on Sustainable Energy*. Custer, WA: Orca Book Publishers, 2013.

Ollhoff, Jim. *Geothermal, Biomass, and Hydrogen*. Minneapolis, MN: Abdo Publishing, 2010.

## Websites

To learn more about Alternative Energy, visit **booklinks.abdopublishing.com**. These links are routinely monitored and updated to provide the most current information available.

Visit **mycorelibrary.com** for free additional tools for teachers and students.

# INDEX

# ABOUT THE AUTHOR

Jodie Mangor has soaked in hot springs in Oregon, Iceland, and Costa Rica. In addition to writing books for children, she also writes audio tour scripts for museums and tourist destinations around the world.